This
Treasure Cove Story
belongs to

**ITTY-BITTY
KITTY RESCUE**

A CENTUM BOOK 978-1-912841-45-5
Published in Great Britain by Centum Books Ltd.
This edition published 2019.

1 3 5 7 9 10 8 6 4 2

Centum Books Ltd, 20 Devon Square, Newton Abbot,
Devon, TQ12 2HR, UK.

www.centumbooksltd.co.uk | books@centumbooksltd.co.uk
CENTUM BOOKS Limited Reg. No. 07641486.

A CIP catalogue record for this book is available
from the British Library.

Printed in China.

Centum

nickelodeon

A Treasure Cove Story

ITTY-BITTY KITTY RESCUE

Based on the screenplay 'Pups and the Kitty-tastrophe'
by Ursula Ziegler Sullivan

Illustrated by Fabrizio Petrossi

It was a warm, sunny day. Chase and Rubble were having a great time playing catch at the beach. Then they heard a far-off cry.

'Meow! Meow!'

A kitten was clinging to a toy boat out in the water!

'Uh-oh!' Rubble exclaimed. 'That little kitty is in trouble.'

'We need to tell Ryder,' Chase said.

Chase and Rubble raced to the Lookout to tell Ryder about the kitty.

'No job is too big, no pup is too small!' declared Ryder. He pushed a button on his PupPad and sounded the PAW Patrol Alarm.

Minutes later, Marshall, Skye, Rocky and Zuma
joined their puppy pals at the Lookout.

'PAW Patrol is ready for action,' reported Chase,
sitting at attention.

'A kitten is floating out to sea,' Ryder announced, pointing to the viewing screen behind him.

'We have to save the itty-bitty kitty!' exclaimed Rubble. Then he straightened up and added, 'I mean, ahem, we have to save the kitten.'

'Zuma, your hovercraft is perfect for a water rescue,'
Ryder said.

'Ready, set, get wet!' Zuma barked.

'And Skye,' Ryder continued, 'I'll need you
and your helicopter to help find the kitten quickly.'

'This pup's got to fly!' Skye exclaimed.

Zuma's hovercraft splashed across Adventure Bay.
Ryder turned his ATV into a Jet Ski and followed.
Up above, Skye zoomed through the air. She quickly
spotted the kitten.

'We're here to help you,' Ryder said, easing his
Jet Ski to a stop.

The little kitten jumped from her boat and landed on Zuma's head. The startled pup fell into the water.

Zuma yelled, 'Don't touch the...'

The kitten accidentally hit the throttle and raced off on the hovercraft.

The hovercraft zoomed around the bay.
Overhead, Skye turned this way and that, trying
to follow the hovercraft's twisting course.
'This kitty is making me dizzy,' she groaned.

Ryder pulled up next to the hovercraft and jumped on board. He stopped the engine and gently picked up the shivering kitten.

'Everything's all right,' he said, pulling a slimy piece of seaweed off the kitten. 'Let's take you back to dry land and get you cleaned up.'

Later that day, Rubble skateboarded into Katie's Pet Parlour with his new BFF. 'Aww, whose cute kitty is that?' Katie asked. 'We don't know,' Rubble explained. 'We found her on the bay with no collar or tags, just this purple ribbon.'

'Does the kitty-widdy
want a nice warm bath?'
Rubble asked.
  'Meow,' the kitten replied.
  'Do you want me to do it?' Katie asked.
'Cats can be a little tricky to bathe.'
'Tricky?' Rubble said. 'Not this little sweetie.'

But the kitten had other ideas. The moment she touched the water, she jumped away with a screech.

She scurried along shelves, knocking over bottles of shampoo.

Rubble slipped on a spinning bottle.

The kitten fell onto Rubble's skateboard
and rolled out the door!

Down the street from Katie's Pet Parlour, Ryder got a message from Rocky: 'A *little girl is looking for her lost kitty named Precious.*'

Ryder recognised the kitten in the picture the girl was holding. Before he could say a word, Precious rolled past on Rubble's skateboard. She skated down a hill and disappeared into town.

'Chase, it's time to use your Super Sniffer!'
Ryder said.

Chase needed something with the kitty's scent
on it. Luckily, they had her purple ribbon.

Chase took a deep sniff. 'She went that way…
ACHOO! Sorry. Cat hair makes me sneeze.'

Sniff, sniff, sniff.

Chase followed the scent until he found Rubble's skateboard at the bottom of the town hall steps.

'Good sniffing,' Ryder said.

Ryder and the pups looked around and saw
a shocking sight.

The kitty was inside the town hall bell tower!

Ryder pulled out his PupPad and called for
Marshall and his fire truck.

'I'm all fired up!' Marshall said as his fire truck screeched to a halt in front of the town hall. He arrived at the same time as the kitty's owner.

Ryder told Marshall to put up his ladder.
'We need to get the kitten down from that tower.'
'I'm on it,' Marshall declared. He extended
the truck's ladder and carefully started to climb.

Marshall reached the top of the ladder.
The scared little kitten was clinging desperately
to a rope in the tower.

'I'll get you down safely,' Marshall said.
'Come here.'

'*Meow,*' Precious whimpered.

The kitten jumped from the rope. She tried to grab Marshall's helmet but missed – and clutched his face instead.

'Whoa!' Marshall yelped. He couldn't see!

The ladder shook. Marshall lost his grip. He and the kitten fell off the ladder!

Ryder caught Marshall, and the little kitty tumbled into her owner's arms.

'Precious!' the girl exclaimed. 'You're okay! You owe these brave pups a thank-you for all their help.'

'Whenever you need us,' Ryder said, 'just yelp for help!'

Treasure Cove Stories

Book list may be subject to change.